MW01041782

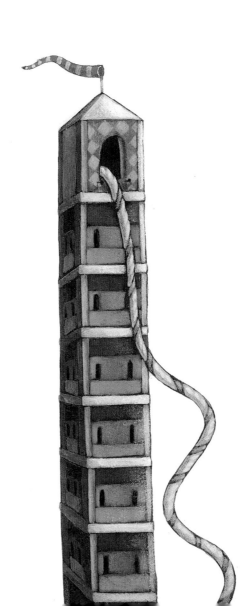

# Rapunzel

*Illustrated by*
*Nicoletta Oeccoli*

*Based upon the story*
*by the Brothers Grimm*

**McGraw-Hill
Children's Publishing**

*McGraw-Hill*
*Children's Publishing*

*A Division of The* **McGraw·Hill** *Companies*

This edition published in the United States in 2002 by
McGraw-Hill Children's Publishing,
A Division of The McGraw-Hill Companies
8787 Orion Place
Columbus, Ohio 43240

www.MHkids.com

ISBN 1-58845-476-2

Library of Congress Cataloging-in-Publication Data is on file with the publisher.

© 2002 Ta Chien Publishing Co., Ltd.
© 2002 Studio Mouse

All rights reserved.  No part of this book may be reproduced or transmitted in
any form or by any means whatsoever without prior written permission of the publisher.

10 9 8 7 6 5 4 3 2 1 CHRT 06 05 04 03 02

Printed in China.

# Rapunzel

Illustrated by
*Nicoletta Oeccoli*

Once upon a time, there was a modest little house tucked snugly inside a green valley. In the house there lived a young couple who longed for a baby of their own.

One day, the woman told her husband that their dearest wish had been granted. She would soon have a child. Her husband was delighted and began to craft a cradle made from the best wood. His young wife stayed in bed to rest, leaving the room only to take in fresh air.

From her balcony, the woman could see into the neighboring garden, which belonged to a powerful witch. Sweet-smelling turnips grew in the center of the witch's beautiful garden. The woman loved turnips and hadn't tasted any in many years. She could think of nothing else.

"Oh, how I wish I could have just one taste of those turnips!" the young woman said, sighing.

In fact, she grew so hungry for the turnips that she found it hard to eat other foods. Her husband worried about her health and that of their baby.

"I will bring you some turnips," he promised.

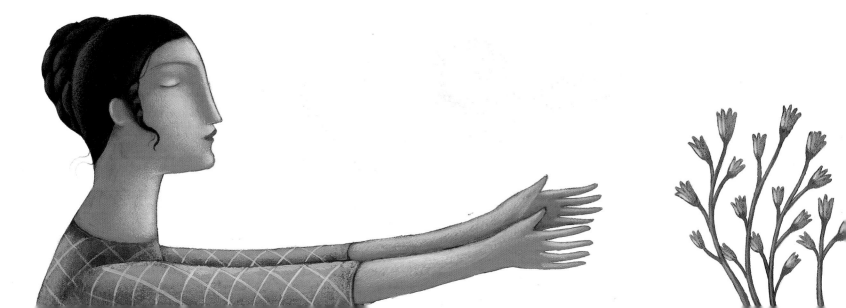

That night, under cover of darkness, the young man climbed over the wall surrounding the witch's garden. He stole handfuls of turnips, put them in a large basket, and brought them home to his wife.

When his wife tasted the turnips, they were even more delicious than she had dreamed.

"Please, my love!" she begged her husband. "I must have more."

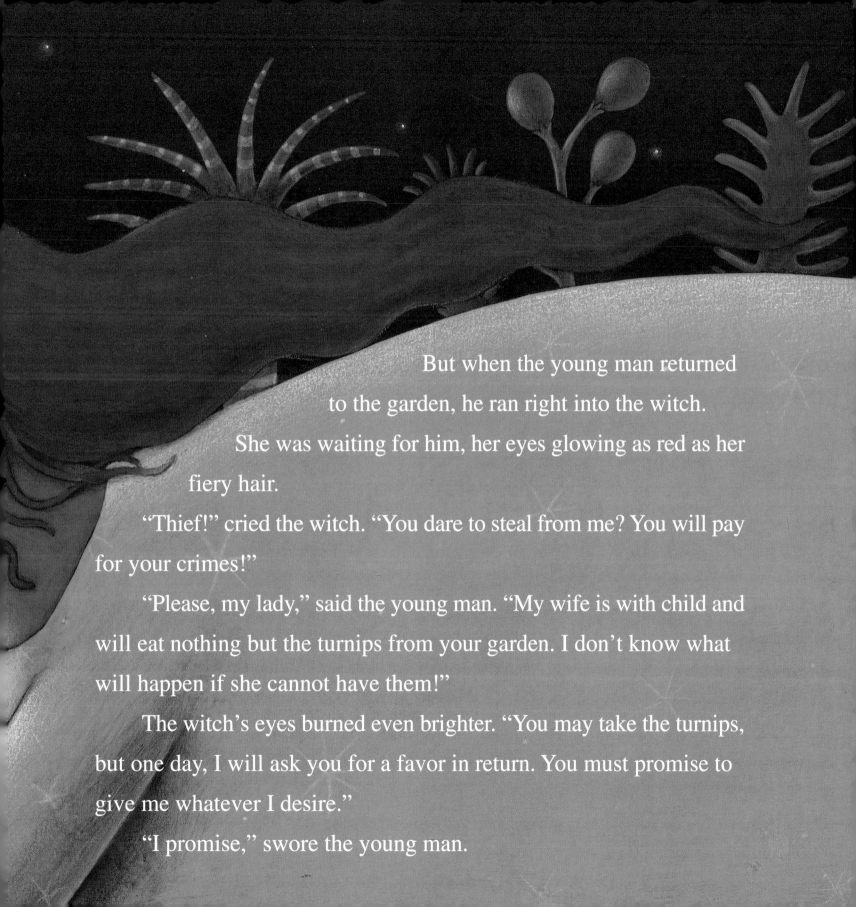

But when the young man returned to the garden, he ran right into the witch.

She was waiting for him, her eyes glowing as red as her fiery hair.

"Thief!" cried the witch. "You dare to steal from me? You will pay for your crimes!"

"Please, my lady," said the young man. "My wife is with child and will eat nothing but the turnips from your garden. I don't know what will happen if she cannot have them!"

The witch's eyes burned even brighter. "You may take the turnips, but one day, I will ask you for a favor in return. You must promise to give me whatever I desire."

"I promise," swore the young man.

Weeks passed, and the young man forgot his promise to the witch. But on the day that his baby girl was born, the witch appeared at the door.

"You owe me a favor," the witch reminded the young man. "Today you must honor your promise."

"I am ready to give you whatever you wish," he said.

The witch pointed to the tiny baby curled in her mother's arms. "That is what I want," she said. "Wrap the baby in a blanket and give her to me."

"No!" cried the young man. "I'll give you anything else you want—anything!"

"Please, don't take our baby!" said his wife, sobbing.

But the witch refused to listen. She snatched the baby from her mother's arms and said, "She will be called Rapunzel." Then she swept out the door, never to be seen again.

As Rapunzel grew, the witch feared that she would run away. To keep her from escaping, the witch hid her from everyone and everything. Then she took Rapunzel to a dark forest and imprisoned her in a tower without a door or any stairs. At the top of the tower was a small window where Rapunzel sat day after day, dreaming of freedom.

When the witch wanted to visit, she called up to the window, "Rapunzel, Rapunzel, let down your hair, so I may climb its golden stair!" And Rapunzel would let her long, golden braid fall to the ground so that the witch could climb up the tower and through the window.

The years passed, and Rapunzel grew into a beautiful, but lonely, young woman. One day, a prince traveling through the forest came upon the strange tower. As the prince moved closer, he saw an evil-looking woman with eyes as red as fire calling out, "Rapunzel, Rapunzel, let down your hair, so I may climb its golden stair."

The prince stayed hidden until the witch had climbed back down the tower and disappeared into the forest. Then he stood at the base of the tower and repeated the witch's words. "Rapunzel, Rapunzel, let down your hair, so I may climb its golden stair!"

When a shimmering, golden braid tumbled to the ground, the prince climbed to the top of the tower.

The prince had never seen anyone so beautiful as Rapunzel, and he instantly fell in love. Rapunzel had never spoken to anyone except the cruel witch, and she was delighted to meet the kind and gentle young prince. When the prince asked to return the next day, she joyfully said that he could.

Rapunzel and her prince met this way for many months, and their love grew stronger each day. For the first time in her life, Rapunzel was happy.

But one day, the witch discovered Rapunzel's secret, and Rapunzel had no choice but to confess.

"Please, forgive me," said Rapunzel, tearfully. "But I love him more than anything."

The witch was furious. She cut off all of Rapunzel's beautiful golden hair and banished her to a desert wasteland where no one would ever find Rapunzel again.

The next day, when the prince called up to the top of the tower, the witch lowered the long golden braid she had cut from Rapunzel's head. When the prince reached the top, he found himself face to face with the evil witch.

"You are wondering what has become of your precious Rapunzel," hissed the witch. "I discovered your secret, and you will never see her again!" And with that, the witch pushed the prince from the tower. He landed in a thorn bush, scratching his eyes so badly that he lost his sight.

For months and months, the prince wandered through the forest, searching for his love. With only the roots of plants to eat and water from cool woodland streams to drink, he survived. But without his lovely Rapunzel, his heart was full of sorrow.

Years passed, and the prince found himself in a desert wasteland. All at once, he felt a breeze that carried a beautiful song. It reminded him of the voice of his Rapunzel.

The prince continued across the sand, hurrying toward the sound. He dared not hope that it could be his one and only love.

Then the song turned to shouts. "My prince! My love!" called
Rapunzel. She ran into his arms, crying with joy. When her tears fell
into the prince's eyes, he was magically healed. He could once more
look upon his true love and feel joy.

With his vision restored, the prince returned to his kingdom with
Rapunzel as his princess. Their love never faded and they lived happily
ever after.

The End

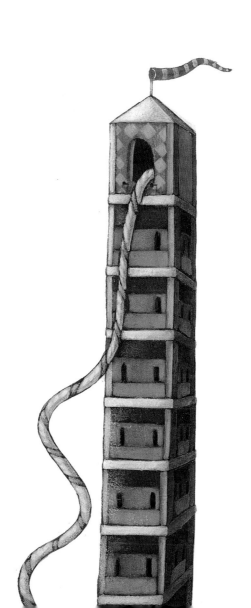